THIS BOOK BELONGS TO:

_____

_____

_____

L IS FOR LOVE.

TO MY AMAZING MOTHER, GRANDMOTHER, AND WIFE,
FOR ALWAYS SUPPORTING MY CREATIVE DREAMS.

FOR EVERY LITTLE AUDRE, AVA, ANGELA, OPRAH,
MALCOLM, MICHELLE, MARTIN, AND MISTY WHO WAS EVER
MADE TO FEEL THAT THEIR BLACKNESS WASN'T BEAUTIFUL.
YOU ARE ENOUGH.

—TR

First published in the USA 2019 by Little Bee Books
First published in the UK 2020 by Macmillan Children's Books
an imprint of Pan Macmillan
The Smithson, 6 Briset Street, London, EC1M 5NR
Associated companies throughout the world
www.panmacmillan.com

ISBN (HB): 9781529062496
ISBN (PB): 9781529062502
ISBN (ebook): 9781529062519

Text and illustrations copyright © Tiffany Rose 2019

The right of Tiffany Rose to be identified as the author and illustrator of this work has been asserted
in accordance with the Copyright, Designs and Patents Act of 1988.

1 3 5 7 9 8 6 4 2

A CIP catalogue record for this book is available from the British Library.

Printed in Spain.

M IS FOR MELANIN

TIFFANY ROSE

MACMILLAN CHILDREN'S BOOKS

is for **AFRO**

Your hair makes a statement.
Embrace the bigness of your hair.
PICK IT, FLUFF IT, LOVE IT.

is for very **BLACK**

Be it unapologetically.

Be bold. Be fearless. **BE YOU.**

is for CREATIVE

Paint the canvas of life with the colours of the rainbow.

Sprinkle your **BLACK GIRL MAGIC** and spread

your **BLACK BOY JOY** around the world.

is for
DREAM

From **MARTIN** to **MICHELLE** and everyone in between, you, little black child, are your ancestors' wildest dream.

is for EMPOWERMENT

If the path you want doesn't exist, **CREATE** it.

Dare to be different. **PERSIST.**

People will say you can't . . . until you do.

is for
FRESH

Our people make something out of
nothing and make it look good.
YOU ARE NO EXCEPTION.

G

is for
GENUINE

There is nothing more honest
than your authentic self.

BE YOU. LOVE YOU. ALWAYS. ALL WAYS.

is for **HIP-HOP**

HIP is knowledge of your culture.
HOP is expression of movement.
DANCE to the music within you.

is for IMAGINE

Imagine yourself as a **BLACK PRIME MINISTER.**
Not just a dream, but a reality to be fulfilled.

is for
JOY

And finding it wherever you look!
IMAGINE, CREATE, INSPIRE . . . the world awaits.

is for
KING

Lift your head high and adjust your crown.
Acknowledge your majesty and act accordingly.

is for
LEAD

Lead with intention and purpose.
YOU WERE NEVER MEANT TO FOLLOW.

is for
MELANIN

Shining in every inch of your skin.
Every **SHADE,** every **HUE.**
All beautiful and unique.

is for **NATURAL**

From your roots to your fingertips.
No additives necessary.
AMAZING. JUST AS YOU ARE.

is for **OBAMA**

The first Black US President.
He **DID,** so that you **CAN.**

is for
PRIDE

Rejoice in who you are and where you come from.
Be present. **STAND TALL, STAND PROUD.**

is for **QUEEN**

MAJESTIC is your mane and sun-kissed is your skin.
ROYALTY flows through your veins.

is for **REMEMBRANCE**

Remember those before you; they
will guide you on your journey.

S

is for
SOUL

NEVER DIMINISH YOUR SHINE so
that others shine brighter.
Be such a **VIBRANT SOUL** that others crave your light.

is for
TRAVEL

A passport is a powerful thing.
To **KNOW THE WORLD** is to better understand yourself.

U
is for
UNLEASH

Unleash your potential; **UNLOCK YOUR MAGIC.**
Put in the work, and see what happens.

is for VOICE

No matter how small, you deserve to be heard.
SPEAK OUT for what is right.
SPEAK UP when others are silent.

is for **WORTHY**

The gifts you'll give to the world
are already within you.
Your worth is not determined by what
you have, but by **WHO YOU ARE.**

is for **MALCOLM**

Activist. Leader. Revolutionary.

Just like Malcolm, **YOU ALONE CAN DEFINE YOU.**

is for YOU

You, _____,
are absolutely ENOUGH.

is for **ZILLION**

There will be a zillion people telling you to do something else or be someone else.
**ALWAYS BE YOUR FREE, TALENTED, QUIRKY, IMAGINATIVE, MELANATED SELF.
THE WORLD WILL ADJUST.**

AUTHOR'S NOTE

Growing up, I never saw books with characters who looked like me, let alone unapologetic blackness. I can't imagine a world in which my children will grow up not seeing a clear mirror of who they are. For so long, black children have been underrepresented in children's literature. It's not just important for black children, but for all children to see a shift in proclaiming the worthiness of all shades to be celebrated.

I created this book for all the children who ever doubted themselves or were made to feel their blackness wasn't enough.

NO MATTER YOUR HUE OR SHADE. THIS IS FOR YOU.

ABOUT THE AUTHOR

Tiffany Rose is a left-handed illustrator and author. She is currently living and working in Georgia, US. She's a lover of coffee, wanderlust, massive curly afros, and children being their imaginative, quirky, free selves. She is a full-time teacher, part-time author-illustrator, and world traveller. Tiffany remembers what it was like as a brown child not seeing herself reflected in the books and characters she loved so dearly, and has been inspired to create art and meaningful stories so that underrepresented children can see themselves in books. Pencil in hand, she's changing that one illustration at a time. ASOUTHPAWDRAWS.COM